Fairy Tale Twists

For my lovely sister, Caroline,
for always making me laugh
K.D.

For Tilly
M.B.

Reading Consultant: Prue Goodwin, Lecturer in literacy and children's books

ORCHARD BOOKS
338 Euston Road, London NW1 3BH
Orchard Books Australia
Level 17/207 Kent Street, Sydney, NSW 2000

First published in 2012
First paperback publication in 2013

ISBN 978 1 40831 213 1 (hardback)
ISBN 97 8 1 40831 221 6 (paperback)

Text © Katie Dale 2012
Illustrations © Matt Buckingham 2012

The rights of Katie Dale to be identified as the author and
Matt Buckingham to be identified as the illustrator of this work
have been asserted by them in accordance
with the Copyright, Designs and Patents Act, 1988.

Fairy Tale Twists

The Wickedest Witch

Written by Katie Dale
Illustrated by Matt Buckingham

ORCHARD

Well, hi there, kids – don't scream, don't flee!
Don't look so scared – it's only me!
I'm not a wicked witch, I swear –
upon my granny's underwear!

I'm never mean, unkind or scary,
honestly – I'm just a fairy!

True, I'm not like most you've seen –
I'm old and ugly (yes, and green).
I've got no wings, I must confess,
no wand or pretty sparkly dress.

The reason is (it's really tragic):
I'm not very good at magic!
All my spells just go amiss…
If not, d'you think I'd look like this?

I haven't always looked this way.
It started on one fateful day...

When I was still at fairy school
and sitting on my small *toad*-stool,
I looked quite normal, but, you see,
I turned bright green with jealousy.

The other fairies were petite,
with little hands and tiny feet.
Their hair grew long in golden curls –
oh, how I envied all those girls!

In desperation at my looks,
I searched in dusty magic books,

and conjured charms and fairy potions,
mystic spells and creams and lotions.

I even tried a beauty curse –
but that just made things ten times worse!

I wished for looks beyond compare –
then sprouted black and wiry hair!

My face swelled up with hairy warts…

My nose grew massive, and all sorts
of pimples broke out on my skin,
then more hair sprouted – on my chin!

I hid myself in sheer disgrace.
I couldn't bear to show my face.

I skipped my classes, skived, rebelled,
till finally I got *ex-spelled*!

And so, because of all these things,
I never earned my fairy wings.
Instead upon a broom I fly,
avoiding dangers in the sky…

There's lightning bolts and thunderstorms,
howling winds and vicious swarms
of bees and wasps, migrating geese –
I hardly get a moment's peace!

But worst of all, the other day,
my buddy Fran was on her way
to see her sister for some tea,
when came the evil Dorothy…

From out of nowhere – wham bam

SPLAT!

Dot's house fell down and squashed her flat!

Then quickly, with no time to lose,
Dot stole the poor old witch's shoes!
(Her favourite scarlet Jimmy Choos!)

Not finished with her witchy slaughter –
then Dot killed Fran's sis – with water!

Having seen these nasty ends,
I've tried to make some mortal friends.
I have to say, it isn't easy –
just my face makes people queasy.
So I had a plan that maybe
I should start with one small baby…

You've heard, of course, of young Aurora,
(pretty girl, but what a snorer!).
When the girl was born, the king
threw an enormous Christening.

(What with the awful post today
my invite must've gone astray,
but still I turned up, nonetheless,
to give my gift of happiness.)

Just then the child began to weep.
She howled and wailed and wouldn't sleep.

No toys could calm the little dear –
but then I had a great idea!

I waved my broom – she stopped her
   screams,
and drifted off to pleasant dreams…

Alas, I got the wording wrong!
It wasn't meant to last so long!
Soon all who knew the little cutie
called the princess "Sleeping Beauty"!

I tried to make amends, but no –
the king was firm – I had to go.
So sadly, and misunderstood,
I went to live within the wood.

I tried to pay for my mistakes
by building houses made of cakes.
So many people lose their way,
they leave the path and go astray.

The woods are dark, the trees are tall,
some never make it out at all.
And so, to keep them warm and fed,
I built a house of gingerbread.

And sure enough, within a week,
two kids, while playing hide-and-seek,
stumbled, lost, into the glade,
and came across the house I'd made.

Their eyes lit up, they rushed inside.
"I've made amends – at last!" I cried.
"Come in!" I beamed, but they just stared.
"Oh no!" I begged them. "Don't be scared!"

"I mean no harm – I swear it's true!
I made this house for kids like you!
To prove it, I'll make any dish –
any cake or treat you wish!"

"Choose anything – go on – go wild!"
The boy looked up and then he smiled.
"I'd really love some cookies, Miss."
"Of course!" I beamed. "Now just
    watch this…"

"Abracadabra! Zing!"

I said,

"Make this young boy gingerbread!"

I clapped my hands and waved my broom

then sweet aromas filled the room.

The house lit up with dazzling light,
the children gasped in sheer delight.
But then the boy, to my surprise,
began to shrink before my eyes!

And as he shrank, his skin began
to turn quite hard, and sort of tan.
His eyes bulged out, his lips went weird.
His nose completely disappeared!

Next went his fingers, then his toes,
and (but for buttons) all his clothes!
"What's happening to me?" he squeaked.
His sister gawped and gasped then shrieked.

"Hans, run!" she screamed, and then she fled.
"She's turned you into gingerbread!"
I watched him flee, I watched her run.
"Oh no!" I wailed. "What have I done?"

"That's it! No magic! No more charms!"
I threw away my useless balms,
my stupid spells and hopeless brew,
and all my books and potions too.

I left it all to start from scratch –
a lonely flat, a veggie patch.
And so I lived a normal life,
free from trouble, pain and strife…

Till one day, tending to my greens,
I found my neighbour stealing beans!

He looked at me, and then he paled.
"Oh, do forgive me, please!" he wailed.
"They're not for me, they're for my daughter.
See, I'm broke! I can't support her –
we're out of bread, of milk and meat;
I've nothing left for her to eat!

"So when I saw your lovely veg,
I couldn't help but hop the hedge!
It's wrong, I'm sorry, look, I'll go—"
"No, wait!" I said. "Hang on a mo'..."

"Take these beans," I told him. "Now, go off to market, buy a cow. With milk and yogurt, cheese and cream, you'll have more food than you could dream!"

"Gee, thanks! But what about my child?"
"I'll babysit for her," I smiled.
He left Rapunzel in my care.
She had the LONGEST golden hair...

…and an ENORMOUS appetite!
(Especially for a little mite.)
She quickly cleaned her dinner plate,
but still she ate and ate and ATE!

She'd soon devoured every crumb
but couldn't fill her hungry tum!
The shelves were bare, the fridge as well.
Oh, how I longed to cast a spell…

But NO! Instead, I locked the door
and rushed to town to *buy* some more.
The roads were bad, the queues were long.
When I got back…

…the girl had gone.

She left a note – she'd met a prince,
and no one's ever seen her since.
Her father didn't understand.
He cursed my name throughout the land.

And so I've done my best, you see,
to hide my true identity.
But still your young perceptive eyes
see what I am through my disguise.

I s'pose I'll always be this way –
old and lonely – what'd you say?
You think I'm wicked? No, I'm not!
Aren't you listening? Sorry, what?

You don't mean "wicked" as in cruel –
But "wicked" as in "Wicked! Cool!"?
You like my "costume", did you say?
It's Halloween? What, now? Today?

Of course I knew! *That's* why I've got
a pointed hat, a cat and pot!
I'm glad you liked my – er, um – *story*.
Not too scary, strange or gory?

Let's go, I'll help you trick or treat
and gather yummy things to eat!
Just hop on board – come on, hold tight!
We could do this every night!

Come, let's be friends – you'll have a ball –
with me – the wickedest witch of all!

Fairy Tale Twists

Written by Katie Dale
Illustrated by Matt Buckingham

All priced at £8.99

Orchard Books are available from all good bookshops,
or can be ordered from our website, www.orchardbooks.co.uk,
or telephone 01235 827702, or fax 01235 827703.